# Matt's Birthday Blessing

The Book of MATT

**Brian Davis** 69 pgs.

Illustrations by Ron Wheeler

McRuffy Press 2003

*To my dad, who taught me
to be a good father.*

Matt's Birthday Blessing

Published by McRuffy Press
PO Box 212
Raymore, Missouri 64083

Story by Brian Davis
Illustrations by Ron Wheeler
Cover design and illustrations by Ron Wheeler

ISBN 1-59269-056-4

www.McRuffy.com

# Contents

# The New Bike

# Chapter 1

# "The Bike of My Dreams"

"Your change is $3.25," said the cashier. Mr. Day picked up the sack and left the counter.

"Matthew, I have the inner tube," Mr. Day spoke to his son. "Come on. We'll be late."

"Dad," answered the boy, "I'm in love."

"What?" questioned the father.

"This is the bike of my dreams," explained the boy. He was looking at a sleek red mountain bike.

Matthew's father laughed, "Just like the video game of your dreams, the sneakers of your dreams..."

The boy joined his father who was already half out the door. "Sneakers! Come on Dad, they were Double Pump Slammers. Anyway, this is better. You wouldn't have to drive me anywhere if I had a bike like that one."

"You were going to run everywhere when I got the sneakers for you. I mean slammers," argued the father. "Besides, I like driving you places."

Matthew got into the car and started to pout. He knew his father wouldn't stand for it long. He was stalling. He needed to come up with a better reason for getting the bike.

"Matthew, the bike you have is perfectly fine. You just need to take better care of it," his father said firmly. Matthew knew his father was done talking about the bike.

The next day, Matthew sat in Sunday School. All he could think about was the new bike. That is, until the teacher started talking about prayer.

"Ask and it shall be given to you..." quoted

Mrs. Taylor. Matthew's hand shot up.

"You mean, I can ask God for anything. Will he give me anything I ask for?"

"Uh... well..." stammered Mrs. Taylor.

"If Jesus said it, isn't it true?" Matthew asked.

Mrs. Taylor sighed, "Well that is what Jesus said, but..."

Just then a few of the parents, brothers, and

sisters started walking through the hallway. They were looking for the rest of their families.

"It's time to go. We'll talk more about this next week," said the teacher.

"Hey, do you want to come over after church?" asked Matthew's friend, Rail.

His friend's real name was Robert. His friends called him Rail because he was as thin as a rail. Robert was sick a lot, so he never gained much weight. He often missed school and most the time he couldn't play. He didn't have too many friends.

Matthew lived on the same block as Rail. They were best friends.

"Hey, maybe we could start working on the treehouse." Rail's eyes lit up at Matthew's suggestion.

They had been planning to build a hideout. They made plans for a treehouse in a big oak tree. They had waited all winter. Now that the days were warmer and longer, they could begin building.

That afternoon the two boys started their quest to find building materials. By mid-afternoon they had a fine collection. They found lumber, tires, and best of all, 3 sheets of metal roofing.

"We're not just building a tree house," said

Matthew proudly. "We're recycling!"

The boys were still making plans when Rail's mom came home.

"Robert!" called his mom as she walked into the kitchen.

"I need to go in now," explained Rail. "She's real tired after working all afternoon at the cafe. I have to help her make supper."

"You cook?" questioned Matthew.

"Like I said, my mom needs my help now that my dad is gone." Rail ran to his back porch. The thin boy opened the door. He looked at Matthew and yelled, "Come back tomorrow. We'll work on the treehouse after school."

"Sure," answered Matthew picking up his dad's hammer. "Tomorrow."

# Chapter 2

# Matthew and Rail

Matthew was a little sad he had to stop working. They were just ready to begin building the treehouse. When Matthew walked through the kitchen door he saw his mom.

"You're home early." she said.

"Rail had to help his mom," explained Matthew.

His mom shook her head. "Imagine, a boy having to help his mom. What will they think of next?" She pointed to the trashcan.

"Very funny," said Matthew as he pulled the bulging plastic bag from the can.

Matthew stuffed the bag into a tall can by the garage. "At least I don't have to cook," he mumbled.

His father walked up behind him. "At least I don't have to eat your cooking." Matthew turned red. He hadn't realized that his dad was

in the garage.

Matthew's bike was turned upside down. "Your tire is all fixed up. You're ready to roll," smiled his dad.

Matthew picked mud off the frame of his bike. "You know, that new bicycle would make a nice birthday present."

His father picked up his tools. "Matthew, you don't need a new bike. We don't have that kind of money right now, anyway."

Matthew just stared at the cement floor of the garage. His father gently pushed Matthew's chin up with a greasy hand. He stared into his son's eyes.

"Besides, we already have your birthday present. I'm sure you're going to like it."

Matthew didn't find his dad's smile that encouraging.

He sat in his room. Sock balls were scattered on the floor.

"Swish!" a sock passed through the tiny basketball goal. "A three pointer at the buzzer! The crowd goes wild!" Matthew danced around the room to act out the victory. "It's a miracle!"

"It's stupid," said his sister as she passed by his bedroom door. Matthew ignored her.

"A miracle," he suddenly had an idea. He knelt by his bed. "Lord, you said in the Bible that we could ask for things. You said you would give us what we pray for. Lord, I want a bike. Amen."

He thought for a second. "I mean, I want the bike I saw in the store yesterday. The red one. In Jesus' name, Amen."

School was boring on Monday. All Matthew could think about was the new bike. Matthew believed he was going to get it. God would tell his parents to buy it for him. Wednesday was his birthday. God would have 48 hours to come through.

"Are you coming over after school?" Rail asked.

"What?" Matthew's mind was still on the bike.

"The treehouse, remember?" Rail looked hurt.

"Oh sure," said Matthew.

The boys put on their jackets. Matthew told Rail about the bike on the way home.

"Sounds awesome!" smiled Rail. "How are you going to get it?"

"I prayed for it," said Matthew proudly.

"You prayed for it? Is that all? I thought you were really getting it."

Matthew stopped and stared at Rail. "Don't you remember what we learned in Sunday School? God answers prayer."

Rail stared at the ground. He kicked loose a half-buried rock. "Maybe we could use this rock in the treehouse?" stated Rail.

He wanted to talk about something different. Matthew was quiet. Rail had never gone to Sunday School until Matthew took him. Rail just didn't understand the Bible like he did.

"If the Bible says it, it's true," explained Matthew.

Rail slumped by the trunk of a tree. "God doesn't answer my prayers."

Matthew sat down next to him. It was then that he noticed the tears in his friend's eyes. "You mean because you get sick a lot?"

Rail was silent. Matthew didn't know what to do.

Rail brushed away a tear. He stared into the air.

"I want a dad," Rail said. Matthew didn't know what to say. Finally Rail stood up. "Let's go build the treehouse."

# Chapter 3

# An Early Birthday Present

Matthew had to go home to change his clothes. "I'll meet you at the tree in fifteen minutes."

Matthew was glad to get away from his friend. But, he also wanted to help him. Matthew ran to his bedroom and changed into his work clothes. He ran from his room.

His mom stopped him at the front door. "Where are you going?"

"To Rail's."

"Be back for supper. Don't forget to bring back your dad's hammer." Matthew started for the door.

"Oh..." his mom stopped him, "someone brought you something today. Maybe it's a birthday card," she said as she pulled a letter from her pocket.

She started to hand it to him. Then she took

it back. "Your birthday isn't until Wednesday. You can wait."

"Oh, please mom...please...please, I want it now," begged Matthew.

Mrs. Day laughed, "Okay, you can open it now."

Matthew wildly tore open the envelope. Nine green pieces of paper floated to the floor. Matthew snatched them up.

"One, two, three, ...eight! Nine ten-dollar bills from Grandma and Grandpa! $90.00, I'm rich!"

His mom had picked up the card. "It says, 'Happy ninth birthday. Here are nine ten-dollar bills. Sorry we'll miss your birthday. Have fun! Love, Grandma and Grandpa.' They came too late to see you this morning. They hoped you would forgive them for missing your birthday."

"They're forgiven!" Matthew stared at the money. "Hey!" his eyes brightened up. "God answered my prayer!"

"What?" asked his mom.

"Yesterday, I prayed for a new bike. I already have some money saved. With this $90.00 I should have enough money to buy it. It's a miracle."

"I'm not sure," argued his mother. "I think you need to pray about how to spend the money. You know how your dad feels about the bike. God's given him wisdom to help you."

"He has to let me get the bike. Don't you see? It's an answered prayer. God wants me to get the bike."

"Let's discuss this with your father."

Matthew was sure his father would agree

with God. "I've got to tell Rail!"

"Okay, but leave the money here," agreed his mom.

Matthew didn't want to lose his fortune. He handed it to his mother.

"I'll put it in a safe place," she assured her

son.

Matthew was out of breath when he reached the tree. It was in the backyard of Rail's house. He expected Rail to be there. "Maybe he got tired of waiting." Matthew started walking to the back door of the house.

A few feet from the door he heard someone crying. This time it wasn't Rail. Rail's mother was crying.

"It's okay, Mom. We'll be okay." Rail was trying to comfort his mother.

Matthew sat on the back step and listened. He knew it was wrong to eavesdrop. This time it seemed to be the right thing to do.

Matthew learned that Rail's mother had lost one of her jobs. She only worked at the cafe on weekends. Her main job was at a clothing store in the mall. The store was going out of business. They wouldn't have enough money to pay their bills.

"Matthew, you know Matthew Day..." Matthew listened more closely when he heard his name. "He told me you can pray. We also learned about it in Sunday School. We can ask God to help us," Rail explained.

His mom hugged him. "Robert, life just doesn't work like that. We need an extra $90.00 just to pay the rent. Money isn't just going to pop into the air."

"I'm going to pray," said Rail. Matthew crept away from the house.

"I'm going to pray, too," Matthew thought to himself.

## Chapter 4

## "Boo!"

That afternoon, Matthew's dad was working on the computer. Mr. Day's back was to the door. Matthew snuck up behind him. He crept closer and closer to the chair.

"Boo!" yelled Matthew, almost in his father's

ear.

Mr. Day jumped, "You're going to get it!"

He grabbed Matthew and started tickling him. Matthew giggled. He rolled onto the floor to get away. Matthew loved sneaking up to his dad.

Mr. Day didn't mind it too bad when Matthew scared him. He liked it even more when he picked on Matthew first. It was like a game. If you asked Matthew, he would say his dad always lost. If you asked Mr. Day, he would say Matthew always lost.

The truth is, they both always won. It was fun. It was a challenge. They would look for creative places to hide.

Later that afternoon, Matthew hid under a pile of laundry. It was piled in his parent's closet. He waited patiently for his father. Mrs. Day was in on it. She asked her husband to get a box off the closet shelf.

Mr. Day flipped on the light. Matthew popped up. Mr. Day got that look on his face. It was the look that said a tickling session was about to begin. Suddenly, Matthew realized he had no place to run.

He was boxed into the closet. There was only one thing Matthew could do. He began pelting his dad with dirty socks. His dad backed off.

"Stinky socks from your stinky feet!" groaned Mr. Day.

He pretended like the smell was choking him. He spun around. Mr. Day plopped onto the bed. He pretended to be overpowered by the smell. Mr. Day closed his eyes and stuck out his

tongue.

Matthew came out of the closet. He started doing a victory dance. Matthew tossed more socks onto his dad. Mr. Day grabbed a pillow. He tossed it at Matthew. The next few minutes were an all-out pillow fight.

"Am I going to have to time you two out?"

threatened Mrs. Day.

"Okay," smiled Mr. Day. "I do need to relax after the battle."

"I was going to have you take a seat on the lawnmower," said Mrs. Day to Mr. Day.

"No, no, we'll be good," pleaded Mr. Day.

"Dad," said Matthew, "Mom helped me scare you. She told you to get the box."

"Hey, that's right," said Mr. Day. "You should be timed out to the lawnmower."

"Only if you do the laundry that you tossed all over this room," said Mrs. Day.

Matthew and Mr. Day looked around the room.

"We'll take the yard," they both agreed.

Matthew and his dad went outside. Mr. Day walked to the tool shed. Matthew followed him. They noticed how tall the grass was getting.

"I have a question," said Matthew.

"No, you can't drive the lawn tractor," said Mr. Day.

"That's not my question," said Matthew. "I want to know if it's possible to pray for a new dad."

"Oh, no! You're not getting rid of me that easily!"

"Not me!" Matthew knew his father was teasing. "I mean Rail. Can God give Rail a new dad?"

Mr. Day thought for a minute, "Do you know what happened to Rail's dad?"

"He doesn't talk about it," said Matthew. "He gets so sad. I don't want to ask."

"Well," said Mr. Day. "God can do anything. Some prayers get answered more quickly than others. We can pray for him. I know it's not God's will for Rail to be sad. He loves Rail."

# Chapter 5

# The Answer

That night, Matthew tossed and turned in his sleep. Finally, he woke up. It was the middle of the night. Matthew got out of bed and walked to his window. He sat down and rested his tired head on the windowsill. The clear, starry sky lit

up the night.

It seemed so huge. God was bigger than the whole sky. If God could create something that great, God could help Rail's mom.

"Lord, will you help Rail's mom? You helped me get a new bike. I know you can do great things."

Nothing seemed to change. Matthew went back to bed. He thought about his friend until he fell asleep.

The next morning something unexpected happened. Matthew opened his sock drawer. Inside was an envelope. It was the $90.00 his grandparents had given him. The money took him by surprise. His mother must have put it there.

Matthew slipped on his blue jeans and a sweatshirt. He stuffed the crisp ten-dollar bills in his pocket.

"You're up early," commented his father.

Matthew ran past him. He almost knocked down his mom as she stepped into the hallway.

"Why do you think he's in such a hurry?" she asked.

"Well, I'd say he's going to get a new bike. Or maybe he set his room on fire," laughed his father.

"Aren't you going to stop him?" asked his mother.

"He's got to learn on his own," said Mr. Day. Then he sniffed the air, "And I don't smell smoke."

Matthew hopped on his bike. He knew time was short. His heart pounded as he peddled as fast as he could. He stopped his bike and jumped off outside of Rail's house. He tried to keep his head lower than the bushes.

Matthew grabbed a pencil from his pocket. He scribbled on the envelope. Matthew plotted his next move. He quietly sneaked up to the house. He could hear Rail and his mother talking.

As silently as he could, Matthew opened the

car door. He pulled the envelope from his pocket. He placed it where it would be seen on the driver's seat. Matthew tried to push the door shut as silently as possible. The door didn't shut all the way, but good enough.

Matthew picked a place in the bushes where he could watch. Rail and his mother came out of the house. Rail's mom looked tired and sad. Matthew smiled.

Rail hopped in the car first. Matthew could see him pick up the envelope. Rail's mother almost sat on it.

"What's this?" asked Rail. Rail's mother looked puzzled.

"I don't know." She stared at it a moment then carefully opened it up.

Matthew watched from behind the bush. He could see the look of joy on their faces.

"What does it say?" asked Rail. His mother had to brush back some tears before she could read.

"It says, here is your rent money. Love, God."

Rail smiled. "Wow! God did answer my prayer. Matthew was right."

# Chapter 6

# It's a Miracle

After the car had left, Matthew got back on his bike. He made it back home in time for school. His sister was already waiting in the car.

"Was the bike shop closed?" joked his father.

"I just needed to see Rail before school."

"Well, next time tell us before you leave."

"Yes, sir," agreed Matthew.

Rail told an amazing story at school. God had answered his prayer with a miracle. Some of the kids thought it was stupid. But, none of them could come up with a better explanation. Other kids thought it was great. Matthew smiled a lot all day, but he didn't talk about the money.

Matthew was in the garage when his dad came home from work. His father had a surprised look on his face.

"What have you done?" were the first words out of his father's mouth. "The glare! The glare!"

His dad shielded his eyes. He pretended to be blinded.

Matthew smiled, "The old bike doesn't look too bad. I washed it," Matthew pointed to the hose. "I even put the hose up when I finished. I used some of your car wax. Mom said it was okay."

"You've done a fine job," said his father. "But, I thought you were getting a new bike."

"I changed my mind."

"Oh, then what are you going to do with all that money?"

Matthew knew he shouldn't lie to his father.

"I don't have it."

"What!" said his wide-eyed father. "Tell me you didn't waste it on a video game."

"I...I gave it away," Matthew didn't know how his father would react. He didn't want to get the money back. Rail's mom needed it.

"I don't understand," questioned his father.

"You know I prayed for a new bike," Matthew began to explain. "When I got the money I thought God wanted me to have it. Then, Rail's mom lost her job.

They didn't have enough money for rent. I put the money in their car. They don't know it was from me."

"Why did you give them all your money?" asked his dad.

"I wanted Rail to believe that God answers prayer." Matthew paused. "There's only one thing that bothers me."

"What's that, son?"

"God didn't answer their prayer, I did."

Matthew's father leaned against the car. "I don't think so."

"What?" asked Matthew.

"You wanted to use the money to buy a bike.

God wanted Rail's mom to have the money. God answered their prayer. You were just being obedient."

"Wow!" said Matthew.

Then, he got a frown on his face. "God didn't answer my prayer. I didn't get a new bike."

"Do you still want the bike?" asked his father. Matthew looked at his shiny old bike.

"Not really. I'm glad I gave the money away."

"Well, son, God did answer your prayer. The Bible says that God gives us the desires of our hearts. Sometimes that means God gives us what we want or need."

"Rail prayed and got exactly what he prayed for, thanks to you. Other times, God changes our hearts. He made you desire to give your money away. Why did you want a new bike?"

Matthew shrugged his shoulders. "I thought it would make me happy."

"Are you happy?" asked his father.

Matthew smiled, "Yes, I am happy. I asked God to make me happy. He did. God did answer my prayer."

Mr. Day gave Matthew a warm hug. His father went into the house. Matthew hopped on his bike. At the end of his driveway Rail rode up on his bike.

Tommy and Rick, two boys from his class were with him. "Cool bike, is it new?" asked the boys.

# Happy Birthday

# Chapter 7

# Happy Birthday

"Happy birthday to you! Happy birthday to you!" sang Matthew's family. He rubbed the sleep from his eyes. His sister and parents came in his room. His mother carried a glowing stack of pancakes. Matthew blew out the nine candles.

"My little boy is another year older!" teased his mom. She kissed him on the cheek.

"Mom! Little boy? I'm nine!"

"You'll always be my little boy even when you're twenty." His mom repeated.

His twelve-year-old sister, Rachel, pinched his cheek. "He's such a darling little boy," she laughed.

"Do you want to live to be thirteen, Rachel?" warned Matthew.

"It's just his way of saying he loves you," Dad said to Rachel.

"Okay, enough of the mushy stuff. Where's the presents?" asked Matthew.

Mr. Day put his hand to his forehead. "Oh, I knew I was forgetting something."

Matthew grabbed his pillow and tossed it at his father. "Last Saturday you told me you already had it."

Matthew laughed as his father tried to think of an answer. Mr. Day started pretending to look for something in his pocket. He pulled an envelope from his pocket and tossed it to Matthew.

Matthew looked puzzled. He felt the fat envelope. It didn't feel like money.

"This is it?"

"Open it," said his mother. Matthew opened the envelope.

Inside was a stack of pictures. He thumbed through them. Each photograph was a different dog. Matthew crinkled his nose.

"Uh thanks, but I don't get it." He was starting to think nine was going to be a long year.

"But you do get it. Any dog you want!" said his mom.

Matthew's face lit up, "Wow!" He stood up on his bed and jumped. His mother grabbed the pancakes as they bounced on the bed.

"We'll take you to the animal shelter," explained his father.

"It's about time. That's where he belongs," teased Rachel.

Matthew grabbed Rachel and tickled her. Giggling, she finally took back what she said. Matthew let Rachel go. She ran from the room laughing.

"Can we go now?" Matthew begged his parents.

"You have school today," explained his mom.

"But, it's my birthday!" protested Matthew.

"And, we want you to have the gift of learning." His father smiled. Matthew didn't always find his dad's humor to be funny.

Matthew's mother explained, "We gave you the pictures to look at today. You can get an idea of the dog you'd like. I'll pick you up from school. Then, we can go to the animal shelter."

Rachel came back with a box. It was wrapped with newspaper. "Save the newspaper. You'll need it if you get a pup."

Matthew read the words on the package out loud. "To my favorite brother."

"I'm your only brother." said Matthew.

"Well you're also my least favorite brother. But it's your birthday. I thought I'd be nice," answered Rachel.

"Wait don't open it yet," said his dad. He

covered his ears. He waited for Rachel and Mrs. Day to cover their ears.

"Okay, you can open it."

"You guys are too funny," said Matthew. But he kept the box away from his face just in case.

Inside the box were a dog dish, an old hairbrush, and a book. Matthew picked up the book. "How To Train Your Dog".

Rachel picked up the brush. "I thought you could use my old brush to comb the dog."

Matthew reached over and gave his sister a hug.

"Thanks!"

# Chapter 8

# A Pup For Matthew

The school day went by slowly. Matthew thumbed through the pictures any chance he got. He was surprised to see his mom at 2:00. She carried a tray of cupcakes. "Oh no," thought Matthew. He was embarrassed. His

mom brought treats for a nine-year-old.

The teacher said, "Everyone put your things away. Mrs. Day has brought treats for Matthew's birthday." Here it comes thought Matthew. His friends were sure to tease him.

Tommy looked at Matthew. "Cool, no spelling!"

"Good work, Matt!" said another boy.

Matthew was a little embarrassed when the class sang "Happy Birthday". Everyone enjoyed the party.

The class cleaned up the cupcake paper, napkins, and cups. "Get your things together!" said Matthew's mom. "We're leaving early."

Matthew could hardly believe it. He was going to get a dog!

"Have you decided on a dog?" asked Rachel.

"No," answered Matthew.

"Well, we're almost there." His mother said as she stopped for a red light. The light changed. Mrs. Day took a left turn. They parked next to a large white building. A sign on the window read, "Second Chance Animal Shelter".

Inside were fenced pens. "Oh, look at the little poodle!" said Rachel.

"I don't think so," said Matthew. He stopped at a pen. "I like this one, and this one."

"You can only pick one," said his mother. "Why don't you pray about it?"

Matthew said a short prayer. He asked God to help him choose the right dog. A third dog began to bark. Matthew went over to the cage. The small, black and white pup licked Matthew's hands.

"This is the one I want."

Matthew took his puppy home. The fuzzy little dog played tag with Matthew and Rachel.

"What are you going to name him?" asked Rachel.

"Buster," answered Matthew.

"Why Buster?" asked Rachel. "I think you should call him Sweet Pea."

"What kind of name is Sweet Pea?" asked

Matthew.

"He's just so sweet. He's also small like a pea," answered Rachel.

"But, he's a dog, not a plant!" said Matthew.

Matthew tossed a stick. Buster ran after the stick. The dog sat by the stick.

"Here Buster! Bring me the stick," yelled Matthew. Buster stood by the stick.

"Bring the stick, Sweet Pea," called Rachel. The dog picked up the stick and ran to Rachel.

Matthew threw the stick again. The dog stopped by the stick.

"Bring it here, Buster," called Matthew. The dog didn't move. Matthew frowned.

Finally he tried, "Bring it here, Sweet Pea." The dog picked up the stick. Buster dropped the stick in Matthew's hand.

"Oh, no!" sighed Matthew.

Matthew threw the stick toward the road. Buster ran after it. The dog was about to pick up the stick. A brown truck drove by slowly. Buster chased the truck and nipped at the tires.

"Come here Buster! Come here Sweet Pea!" the children yelled.

The truck sped up and drove away. Buster stood panting at the corner of the yard. His tongue flapped in the wind.

"Bad dog!" yelled Matthew as he grabbed Buster's collar. Buster lowered his head and tucked his tail in between his legs.

BAD DOG!

"I think you hurt his feelings," said Rachel.

"Well he's got to learn not to chase cars," said Matthew.

"Dinner time!" called their mother from the back door of the house.

Matthew put Buster on a leash. He tied him to a tree and made sure Buster had fresh water. Matthew stared at the dog. Buster didn't seem nearly as cheerful after being yelled at.

Matthew felt a strange feeling inside. He felt hurt and sorry he had yelled at Buster. At the same time, he knew he had done the right thing.

# Chapter 9

# Obedience Training

The next morning rain was pouring down. Matthew was glad he had put Buster in the garage after supper.

"Looks like you better wear your boots to school," said his mother.

"No way, I'll get laughed off the bus," said Matthew.

"I'm wearing mine," said Rachel as she walked by wearing her pink boots.

Matthew's were bright blue with puppy dogs on them. Two years ago they were okay. Now he was nine. Actually, he didn't dislike the boots that much. He just didn't like to be teased about them.

"Matthew, I don't want you to have wet feet all day. I don't want you coming down with a cold. Now, go to your room and get your boots. You can wear your sneakers...I mean slammers when you get to school," said his mother.

Matthew came back wearing the blue boots.

He carried another pair of shoes in his hands. His mother gave him a plastic bag to keep the other shoes dry.

"Rachel's already waiting at the bus stop. Now hurry!"

Matthew stepped out the door. He stood on the front step under the roof. He knew his mother wouldn't be watching. He quickly slipped off the boots. Next, he put on the tennis shoes. Matthew tossed the boots in the garage and ran for the bus.

When he got to the bus Rachel asked, "Where's your boots?"

"They didn't fit anymore, so I had to wear these," lied Matthew.

"I don't believe you! I'm going to tell Mom." She started to walk back toward their house.

"The bus is coming!" yelled Matthew.

The bus turned the corner and splashed up the street. Matthew laughed as his sister made a mad dash to the bus.

"Serves her right!" he thought to himself. "Oh!"

Cold water sunk into his shoe as he stepped

toward the bus. He had been too busy watching Rachel. He didn't notice the puddle until both feet were soaked.

Having wet slushy feet made Matthew's day terrible. Having lied didn't make him feel any better. "Maybe being teased wouldn't have been so bad," he thought. He watched thesecond hand on the clock tick. He was twenty minutes away from the end of school.

Matthew walked to the bus after the class was dismissed.

"Nice boots," called Rachel as he neared the bus.

"Oh no," Matthew thought to himself. He had hoped she had forgotten. "They're my feet and my shoes! I can wear what I want," Matthew said angrily.

"I bet Mom doesn't think so!" answered Rachel.

"I bet she doesn't like you wearing her lipstick either!" threatened Matthew.

"How did you know about that?" Rachel

turned pale.

"I emptied the trash cans in the house last week. Lip prints all over tissue paper. Big mouth lip prints...had to be yours."

Rachel turned pale. "You're not going to tell?"

"Of course not. Do unto others as you would have them do unto you." Matthew smiled.

"Okay," said Rachel, "but I'm not going to lie for you."

As soon as Matthew got home he changed into dry shoes. He tossed the wet shoes and socks in his closet. His shriveled toes enjoyed the warmth of dry socks.

"I've really got to get Dad to buy me new boots."

The rain had stopped earlier that day. Buster was glad to see Matthew. Matthew's mom had bought Buster some doggy treats. His dad had told him to use them as rewards. Every time Buster answered to his name, he got a treat.

Matthew let Buster out of the garage. He let Buster sniff a treat. The dog licked his lips and danced happily.

"Stay!" commanded Matthew as he backed away from the dog. After he was a few feet away, he called, "Here Buster." The dog looked puzzled.

Matthew waved the doggy treat. "Here, Buster!" This time, the dog came. Matthew gave the dog the treat and a big hug. "Good, Buster!" Matthew repeated this several times.

Sometimes the dog got a treat. Sometimes the dog just got a hug. Buster seemed happy to get either one.

Next, Matthew threw a stick. Buster chased it and grabbed it in his mouth.

"Here Buster! Bring the stick here!" Buster ran to him. "Thank you, God!" Matthew was grateful not to have to call his dog Sweat Pea.

A car turned the corner and came down the street. Buster jumped up from beside Matthew and chased the car. This time the car was coming toward Buster.

"No! Stop!" yelled Matthew. Matthew closed his eyes as he heard the tires screech to a stop.

"You better keep that dog in the yard!" A man yelled from the car.

SCREEEECH!!!

Matthew opened his eyes and saw Buster sniffing at the tires.

"Here Buster!" Matthew grabbed the dog's collar and pulled him away. The man very carefully drove off.

"Bad dog! You could have gotten ran over! No more doggy treats today!"

Just then another car passed by. Buster jumped and Matthew fell over backwards. Buster landed on top of him.

"That's it!" yelled Matthew. He dragged Buster to the tree and snapped the leash on the collar. "You'll have to stay tied up until you learn to follow directions."

# Chapter 10

# Buster's Bad Habit

Matthew told his parents about his problem with Buster at dinner. His father had already been working on a solution. He had planned to put up a fence in the backyard.

"All I need to do is put a fence between our house and the neighbor's fence. Their fences already surround us. I've been meaning to do it anyway. You should also keep trying to teach Buster to do what you say."

"Yes," said his mother. "You should expect Buster to obey you. You know what is best for him." She stared right at Matthew.

Matthew suddenly had a sinking feeling.

"Okay, okay, I used your lipstick! How did you find out?" cried Rachel.

Her mother and father both looked surprised. "What are you talking about Rachel?" asked her mother.

"Uh..." Rachel realized she had just told on herself.

Matthew knew she would tell on him next. But, he had a feeling it wouldn't matter.

"You know, don't you?" he asked his parents. His mother pulled a sack from under the table.

She pulled out two mangled pieces of blue rubber. "You need to teach Buster not to chew boots," she said.

"I...I," said Matthew, "I'm sorry." He felt like Buster after being scolded. He wanted to tuck his tail and crawl under the table.

"What are you going to do to us?"

asked Rachel sheepishly.

"We're going to put you on a leash and tie you to a tree. Just like Buster!" said her father.

"What? Tie us to a tree?" said Rachel, "That's child abuse!"

"What your father means, is that you're grounded. Just like Buster can't run off. You won't be able to run off and play for two weeks."

"That's not fair!" said Rachel.

"Yes it is," said Matthew quietly.

"What?" said his father, "Do I need to have my ears checked? Did you say you should be punished?"

"Your ears are fine. Dad, do you enjoy punishing us?" asked Matthew.

"There's nothing I like less," answered his father.

"Then why do you do it?" asked Rachel.

"I know," said Matthew. "When Buster chased cars, I wanted to stop him. When I yelled at him I felt bad. He was happy, and I made him sad. I had to punish him. He had to learn. It was wrong for me to not wear my boots. It was wrong for you to use Mom's lipstick."

"That's partly true, Matthew," said his father. "That's not the only way you learn. Sometimes we get to reward you for doing things well. We enjoy doing that."

"Like giving Buster doggy treats!" said Matthew.

"That's right. But you also need to understand how you were wrong. Not wearing boots isn't the only problem. Wearing lipstick wasn't the only thing Rachel did wrong. You disobeyed your mother. That's what was wrong. That's why you're being disciplined."

"Disa what?" asked Matthew.

"Disciplined. It means to train your mind. We want you to grow up and be able to make good decisions."

"I can't wait until I grow up. Then I won't need to be disa...disa...grounded." said Rachel.

"Well, we still get disciplined," said her father.

"By who?" asked Matthew.

"By Mom," answered Rachel.

Mrs. Day laughed, "That's too big of a job for me. I try to leave that up to God."

"That's right," smiled Mr. Day. "It says in the Bible that God disciplines His children."

"Don't look now, Dad, but you're not a child," said Matthew.

"But, Mom does say you're just a big kid sometimes," said Rachel.

Mr. Day shook his head. "We're all God's children. You'll always be our children even when you're really old."

"Like forty?" grinned Rachel.

"Okay, let's be serious for just one more minute," said Mr. Day. "I'm trying to explain that sometimes things don't go the way we want them. I have to pray about those things. God shows me where I was wrong.

God is disciplining me. It helps me learn to obey Him. It's a good thing to be disciplined. It shows that God loves us and wants to protect us."

"I see," said Matthew. "If I don't discipline

Buster, he could get ran over."

"Right," said his mother. "If you're not disciplined you would think it was alright to disobey. You could end up sick or hurt."

"You mean, you're grounding us because you love us!" said Rachel.

"Right," said her mom.

"Then you can ground us for three weeks. I know you love us a lot!" said Matthew.

"Not me! Being grounded two weeks is all the love I need," said Rachel.

Everyone laughed.

# Chapter 11

# The Boots

The car began slowing as it neared Matthew. His eyes were not on the car. He was watching Buster. The dog started to get excited about the oncoming car. He danced his little puppy dance.

Matthew had a hard time not laughing. He resisted the temptation. Buster needed to know that Matthew was serious. Chasing cars was not a healthy thing for his pup to do.

The car door opened. Rail stepped out. Buster could hardly contain himself. His puppy dog eyes stared up at Matthew. Matthew smiled and nodded, "Go get him!"

Buster didn't need to be asked twice. He ran to greet Rail. The pup licked the boy's face like a popsicle on a hot summer day. Rail gave the pup a hug in return.

Matthew was glad he was no longer grounded. He needed some quality play time. It

had been two weeks since he had seen his friend. Actually, he had seen Rail everyday. School didn't count.

Being grounded was tough. Matthew was going to be careful not to have that happen again. Buster had learned a lot in two weeks, too. The pup had passed the test today. He didn't chase the car.

Rail's mom got out of the car. She pulled a bag out of the back seat. Rail ran to her side. He had a big smile on his face.

"This is just for you," said Rail's mom to Matthew.

"Why?" asked Matthew.

"It's a birthday present," said Rail. "I know

it's a little late. But…"

"Robert has been working very hard for this," said Rail's mom. "He's been helping all our neighbors and earning money."

Rail's face was turning red. He was a little embarrassed. "Well, I didn't have much to do anyway. Life gets boring fast when you're grounded, Matt."

"I'll try not to let it happen again," smiled Matthew. "Believe me. I've learned all about being bored."

Matthew looked at Rail. His friend was so excited to give the gift. It actually made Matthew feel a little funny. He knew Rail and his mom needed all the money they could get. That meant more to him than whatever was in the bag.

"Well, open it!" ordered Rail. He had waited two weeks for this moment.

Matthew opened the bag. He reached through the tissue paper. His hand brushed against something rubbery. Matthew pulled.

Out came a pair of brand new boots. They weren't bright blue. They didn't have puppy dogs on them. They were a nice black with brown trim. They were perfect for a nine-year-old boy.

Rail grabbed a boot, "They have a pull-out

lining. You can wear them in the summer or winter. Plus, no one will laugh at you when you wear them."

"That's a big plus."

"Robert didn't want you to get grounded again for not wearing boots," explained Rail's mom.

"He picked them out himself. He was afraid I would get you something that wasn't cool. I'm not sure he did a good job. They look warm to me."

"Mom!"

"Just kidding," smiled Rail's mom.

Matthew returned the smile. It was the first time he had heard Rail's mom joke about anything. She had always seemed sad or tired.

She seemed as happy as Rail to give the gift.

"Do you like them?" asked Rail.

"They're great," said Matthew. "Bring on the rain! Thanks, Rail. I'll make sure my other birthday present doesn't eat them." Matthew patted Buster on the head.

# Chapter 12

# Moms Always Know

Matthew had hoped Rail could stay. Rail was on his way out of town for the weekend. They were going to his grandmother's house. Matthew was disappointed. He didn't let it show. Rail was too happy.

Matthew didn't want to spoil the moment. He watched the car drive away. Buster stayed by his side. The pup thought about chasing the car. He whined softly.

Matthew carried the boots back to the house. The front door bumped a ladder as he opened it. Matthew peaked around the door. His mother was changing a light bulb.

She climbed down. Matthew slipped through the doorway.

"I see you got the boots," said Mrs. Day.

"You knew about this?" asked Matthew.

"Moms know everything," she smiled. "Okay, I was in the store when they bought them. They asked me what size you wore. Do you like the boots?"

"Yes, they're great but…"

"It's not quite the gift you would expect from a friend?" Mrs. Day seemed to know just what he was thinking.

Matthew nodded.

Mrs. Day looked her son in the eye, "When Rail gets a new shirt, new jeans or anything, he really appreciates it. He knows how hard his

mother worked to get it for him."

"That's just it," said Matthew. "Rail worked

two weeks for these boots. There are lots of things he could have gotten for himself. There are so many things he really needs. He gave everything he had for me."

Mrs. Day gave her son a hug. "I think you're learning what a good friend he is. He could have gotten you a toy, but he knows you have lots of toys. He knew you needed boots."

"I'm really grateful for everything I got for my birthday."

"That reminds me," said Mrs. Day. "Your grandparents are back in town. Have you written your thank-you letter to them?"

"No," said Matthew. "But, I'm in a real thankful mood."

"You can write the letter and stuff it in the envelope on the desk. There's a note from me in there too."

Matthew wrote the thank you letter to his grandparents. He also wrote one to Rail. He folded the first letter and began to place it in the envelope. He saw his mom's note. There was something else in there. It was a photograph.

Matthew pulled it out. He couldn't believe his eyes. It was a picture of Rachel. His sister was staring in a mirror. She was putting on lipstick. Matthew needed an explanation. He took the photograph to his mom.

"What's this?"

Mrs. Day smiled, "That's Rachel."

Matthew sighed, "I know that. Do you see what she's doing? Didn't she learn anything from being grounded?"

"I took this before she was grounded," said his mother.

"Before?" Matthew couldn't believe what he was hearing. "I didn't think you knew. It's like you're everywhere. You were there when Rail bought my boots. You were there when Rachel wore lipstick. It's like they say God is…omni…"

"Omnipresent," said Mrs. Day. "God is present everywhere. He's omnipresent. I'm not omnipresent."

"Maybe not," said Matthew. "But you sure are momma-present!"

***The Book of Matt*** is a chapter book series from McRuffy Press that emphasizes Christian values in a fresh and creative way.

### Matt's Birthday Blessing

Turning nine is just fine with Matthew Day. He's picked out a special birthday presnt, and knows how to get it. With God on his side, he can't go wrong. Or can he be?

ISBN 1-59269-056-4

### My Shoes Got the Blues

What do a bulldog, a basketall star, and a big race have in common? They're all reasons Matthew's shoes have the blues. His Double Pump Slammers will never be the same.

ISBN 1-59269-057-2

### Matthew and Goliath

Big problems somtimes need small solutions. When Nathan Goliath moves to town, there's nothing but trouble, big trouble. Can one small boy stop the bullying?

ISBN 1-59269-058-0

## About the author...

Brian Davis is a former school teacher. He has a Master's Degree in Reading instruction. He is the author of several reading, phonics, and math curricula, as well as other children's stories.

Brian and his wife, Sherylynn, have a daughter named Hannah, and a son named Matthew, who is still waiting for his "Buster".

## About the illustrator...

You can find more of Ron Wheeler's work at his website:
www.cartoonworks.com

Visit **www.McRuffy.com** for more
McRuffy Press products.

Find out the lastest about the Book of Matt at
**www.TheBookofMatt.com**